BEOWULF

KINGFISHER EPICS

BEOWULF

Retold by PENELOPE HICKS

Illustrated by
JAMES McLEAN

KINGFISHER
BOSTON

For Sophie and Jack, with love—**P. H.**

For Chrissie, Jane, Laura, Mary, and Dirk—**J. M.**

KINGFISHER
a Houghton Mifflin Company imprint
222 Berkeley Street
Boston, Massachusetts 02116
www.houghtonmifflinbooks.com

First published in 2007
2 4 6 8 10 9 7 5 3 1

LIBRARY OF CONGRESS CATALOGING-IN-PUBLICATION DATA
has been applied for.

ISBN 978-0-7534-6134-1

Printed in India
1TR/0407/THOM(PICA)/120BILTS/C

CONTENTS

PROLOGUE

isten!

The world was black. Thunderclouds had built up in the sky, threatening the land with the coming storm and throwing dark shadows over the sea. Daylight struggled to break through the clouds, and the tops of the waves showed no sparkle of sunshine. Needles of sleet fell on the sea birds as they tossed above the water with their widespread wings. Birds were the only moving creatures to be seen, and they lived without fear in this friendless, storm-beaten world.

Where the land met the sea, a tall cliff rose straight up from the thrashing water. At the foot of this cliff was a small stretch of beach, now filled with the surging water, then left bare as the strong tides swept the water backward and forward over the scattered rocks. On the cliff top stood a man, huddled in a cloak and leaning on his spear. He was a guard, watching from a high position for any enemies who might approach his land—the land of the Spear-Danes.

After a few minutes the man stirred, conscious of the piercing chill, shifted his position. He walked a step or two along the cliff top, stamping his feet in an attempt to stay warm. His gaze constantly swept across the angry sea, but there was nothing to see except the churning water; nothing to hear except the wind, the waves, and the screaming voices of the sea birds.

Then a flash of lightning zigzagged across the sky, followed by a deep rumble of thunder. The guard suddenly stiffened. He narrowed his eyes as he leaned forward and peered through the icy sleet toward the bottom of the cliff. Something was down there! He wasn't sure what he had seen, and for a moment he thought that he was mistaken. But then, again, he saw it. A small boat, barely more than the length of two men and with a single sail, was being driven in toward the stretch of beach. The guard watched as it spun in the surf, its sail flapping wildly. Then he saw it suddenly still, poised for a moment on the crest of a giant wave. As the guard stared down, waiting for the boat to disappear into the swirling waters, the wave broke, and the small vessel was hurled by the fierce current down toward the tumbled rocks at the bottom of the cliff.

Uncertain what to do next, the guard continued to watch from the cliff top. Where had the boat come from? Had it survived? Was there anybody in it? The guard didn't know the answer to any of the questions that rushed through his mind. Again and again, the waves broke against the cliff, and the spray filled the air, blocking his view. Then for a moment the waves fell back, and the boat was suddenly clearly visible, rocking violently among the boulders at the water's edge.

The watching man drew in his breath with a hissing sound; there was something about the ice-covered, curved prow of the boat that stirred him in a way that he did not understand. He turned away from the cliff's edge and hurried toward a path that wound down from the top to the sea below. Pushing against the blustering wind and rain, with his cloak tightly clutched around him, he made his way to the beach.

As he approached the boat, the guard held his spear in front of him, ready to fight if it would be necessary. He felt a chill run down his spine, different from the cold of the storm—a chill that told him that this was a moment

of destiny. Before him stood a child, draped in a cloak of rough skins, upright and unafraid in the center of the boat.

What can this mean? the guard wondered. *A child, alone on the open seas. Where has he come from? Who has sent him to our land?*

The guard hurried to the boat, splashing through the water to reach the child. He lifted out the boy and quickly wrapped him in his own cloak.

"Don't be afraid," he spoke gently. "You're safe now. What's your name?"

But the boy didn't answer. He just stared up at the man with fearless, wide blue eyes. The guard thought that it was best to return to his people, where the child could be taken care of. He cradled the boy in his arms, labored back up the cliff, and hurried toward his village.

That is how the boy Shield Sheafing first came to the land of the Spear-Danes. He never told his story about where he had come from, why he was alone in an open boat, or who had sent him. But this mysterious boy, without family or land, came at a time when the Spear-Danes were without a king. They were drifting without a leader, as the child himself had drifted in a boat across the great sea.

Shield Sheafing grew up in the land of the Spear-Danes and brought them prosperity and fame. Over the years he was honored and obeyed, and in time he was chosen to be their king. He married a beautiful young Spear-Dane woman, and they had a son. Then, after many years of prosperous rule, Shield Sheafing died. His spirit moved to the heavens, and his body was carried to the water's edge. His loyal thanes filled a ship with treasures of twisted gold, battle swords, and spun-gold banners. Shield Sheafing's body was placed gently in the midst of these treasures. He had come to this land of the Spear-Danes alone and homeless. Now he left as alone as he had been then, but this time he was surrounded by riches.

The ship was pushed out to sea. The tide slowly caught it and carried the ship away, over the waves. Shield Sheafing was leaving the land of the Spear-Danes as silently and mysteriously as when he had arrived as a child all those years ago.

THE MONSTER

In the wild lands beyond the homes of the Spear-Danes a grim and powerful monster lived in the darkness. The creature's shape was not unlike a man's, but his hideous head was sunk between his hunched shoulders and his eyes were set deep into his skull. His lipless mouth was wide with sharp and vicious teeth. His matted hair smelled foul, and his skin was blistered with festering sores. His long arms hung loosely at his sides. On each hand and foot were curved and terrible iron claws. During the day, when the sky was filled with light, he would stay hidden away in the marshes.

He hated the brightness and preferred to stay hidden from the sight of humans. But when night fell, he would creep out from his lair and sniff the air like an animal, peering around to make sure that he wasn't seen. Then he would go hunting, killing anything or anyone in his way. This evil creature lived a savage life. His name was Grendel.

Hrothgar, the great-grandson of Shield Sheafing, was now the king of the Spear-Danes. Like his ancestor, he was a wise and much- loved king. Under his rule, the Spear-Danes had become happy and

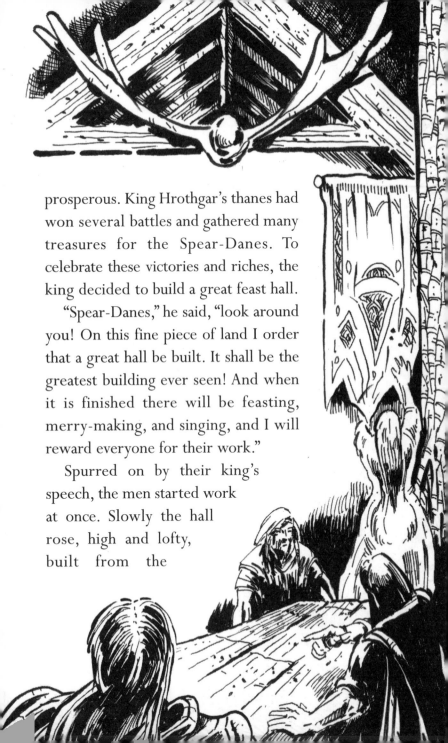

prosperous. King Hrothgar's thanes had won several battles and gathered many treasures for the Spear-Danes. To celebrate these victories and riches, the king decided to build a great feast hall.

"Spear-Danes," he said, "look around you! On this fine piece of land I order that a great hall be built. It shall be the greatest building ever seen! And when it is finished there will be feasting, merry-making, and singing, and I will reward everyone for their work."

Spurred on by their king's speech, the men started work at once. Slowly the hall rose, high and lofty, built from the

strongest trees in the forests.

"Men from other lands will marvel at our hall!" they proclaimed.

When the building was finished, the feast hall was decorated with spun-gold banners lining the walls. Golden cups and bowls were brought to the hall and placed on the long table that stood at the head of the hall. Attached to to the roof gables was a pair of stag's antlers. The hall was named "Heorot," which meant "stag."

King Hrothgar called everyone to Heorot for a great feast and an evening of merry making. The hall smelled of roasting meats from the open spit and of strong mead brewed from

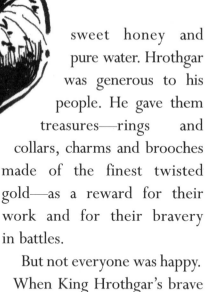

sweet honey and pure water. Hrothgar was generous to his people. He gave them treasures—rings and collars, charms and brooches made of the finest twisted gold—as a reward for their work and for their bravery in battles.

But not everyone was happy. When King Hrothgar's brave warriors sang about victory in the great feast hall, their voices and the music from the minstrels' harps echoed over the lands until it reached the monster Grendel's lair. Grendel hated hearing the laughter and singing. He hated the happiness and friendship of the Spear-Dane warriors. His hatred grew so strong that he could bear it no longer.

One night, under the cover

18

of darkness, he silently stalked from his marshy lair to Heorot. He crouched in the darkness, spying on the Spear-Danes and loathing them for the happiness that they were enjoying. After this first secret visit, he grew bolder, and on many nights he would creep up to Heorot's door. Slowly his anger and hatred grew until he decided that he would destroy the feast hall and all the people within it.

BEOWULF, THE BOY

In a neighboring land, the land of the Geats, there lived a boy named Beowulf. His father was a great warlord, and his mother was the sister of Hygelac, the king of the Geats. Beowulf had been sent to live in his uncle's court where he grew up to be a fearless fighter, popular with all of the other young thanes. But some of the older men in the court didn't like the young nobleman. They were jealous of his friendship with the king and didn't like his position in the court. They spread rumors, saying that Beowulf was a weakling and not a worthy prince.

Beowulf wasn't happy when he found out that people were laughing at him behind his back. He knew that he was strong and not afraid of anything. He decided that he had to prove it, to show them how wrong they were.

His greatest friend was Breca, a lively young thane who loved adventures. One day Beowulf spoke quietly to his friend.

"Breca, I need to prove to these idle gossipers that they're wrong to laugh at me. Will you help me? I want to show all the Geats that I'm no weakling!"

Breca laughed. "Of course! Let's seek adventure! Beowulf, I challenge you to a swimming contest. Let's see who can swim in the sea for the longest time and who can go the farthest."

"And if we meet any sea monsters, we'll fight them together with our swords!" replied Beowulf excitedly. "We'll see who can overcome the most until we return to land."

The two friends strapped their mighty swords to their sides and plunged into the waves. For the first day they swam easily, side by side in the water, laughing at their strength. On the second day, just as the sun was

rising in the east, Beowulf saw a surge in the water a
short distance ahead of him.

"Look out, Breca!" he cried. "There's some kind
of sea creature nearby!"

The two young men quickly pulled their swords
free and trod water, ready to fight if necessary. They
saw a huge serpent's head, foam-flecked and hideous,
rear up out of the waves. They knew that they would
have to fight for their lives. As the serpent sped through
the water toward them, Beowulf and Breca separated.
The serpent didn't know which one to attack first. At

the last moment it swerved toward Beowulf, but he was ready for it. As the serpent's terrible jaws opened to grab him, Beowulf struck one mighty blow at the foul head. Blood gushed from the serpent's body, staining the sea before it sank into the depths.

Breca shouted and waved his sword with joy. "Well fought, Beowulf!" he called. "The first victory is to you!"

For two more days and nights the friends swam together, sometimes trying to outdo one another in speed but always staying close together in the waves. Breca would suddenly surge ahead of his friend, challenging Beowulf to catch him. Beowulf would immediately chase after Breca and grab him by his legs, so that the two tussled and laughed together in the sea, as they had done many times on land.

On the fourth day, still not feeling tired, they saw another evil creature, and this time Breca attacked it. Beowulf watched as the creature's blood spurted over his friend's arms and shoulders. But in spite of its wounds, the monster was too strong for Breca, and Beowulf saw that his friend was in terrible danger.

"Hold on!" he shouted. "I'll help you."

He swam quickly toward Breca, and the two friends fought side by side. Now the foul monster turned on Beowulf, grabbing him and dragging him deep under the water. But Beowulf would not surrender. He turned the point of his sword and thrust it with all of his strength into the monster's neck. Dark blood from the defeated creature seeped into the water, as Beowulf shook himself free from its clutches and swam to the surface again.

Once again the two friends shouted out in victory. Beowulf and Breca met and defeated more sea monsters that day. They both knew that it was Beowulf's strength and skills that kept them alive.

On the fifth day of the swim the two friends were met by strong currents and a rising storm. They could not defeat these with their swords. No matter how much they tried, they were unable to stay together. Swiftly they were swept apart.

Beowulf saw his friend's head

bobbing in the waves. "Breca, take care of yourself!" he called out. "Don't give up!"

Breca raised an arm. "If it's our fate, we will meet again!" he shouted, battling with the currents.

Then the two lost sight of each other in the huge ocean. Beowulf forced himself not to think about his friend as he fought against the waves and struggled toward the distant land.

Two days later Beowulf staggered onto a deserted and storm-beaten shore. He was exhausted but proud that he had survived. When he had recovered his breath, he made his way across the land to find out where the surging tides had carried him. The people he met were astonished by his story and gave him food and fresh clothes. They told him that he was far to the north of his homeland, the land of the Geats. Beowulf made his way across the countryside until he reached his own people. As he approached the great hall where his uncle, King Hygelac, would be, he saw Breca.

"Breca!" He could scarcely believe his eyes. The two young men embraced joyfully.

"Well, Beowulf, my friend. I didn't expect to see you again!" Breca patted him on the shoulder and told him how he had reached the safety of land in the south.

When the Geats heard the story of the two

friends' great adventure—swimming for seven days and seven nights in the sea—and of the sea monsters that they had defeated, they all agreed that these were two exceptional young men. No longer did some of the older thanes mutter anything against Beowulf. He was now recognized as a true and mighty prince, bold enough to fight any enemy in a battle!

GRENDEL ATTACKS

One night, when the clouds covered the sky over the land of the Spear-Danes, hiding the moon's light, Grendel set out for Heorot, the great feast hall. The monster had decided that tonight he would attack and destroy the unsuspecting Spear-Danes. Unseen, he crouched in the darkness and waited. As the sound of laughter and music died down, he approached the huge wooden door. He pushed it open and peered into the great hall.

Inside the light was dim. Flickering torches on the walls threw long black shadows across the giant room. But Grendel's eyes were used to darkness, and he had no trouble seeing the sleeping warriors, wrapped in their cloaks, lying along each side of the hall. Some lay on benches; others lay on the rush-covered floor. Grendel showed no mercy. Quickly, and with scarcely a sound, he trod on his massive clawed feet through the door and into the hall. Grendel looked around in fury. Then, with a terrible and savage speed, he fell upon the closest thanes. He seized, tore to pieces, and ate 30 of them before they could reach for their swords.

The terrible sounds woke the other men, but they were too shocked and slow to save their friends.

Grendel, now glutted by his slaughter, sped away to his lair in the swamps.

"Look! There's a pile of blood-covered bones by the door!" one thane cried in horror as he peered around the dimly lit hall.

"See the blood-spattered floors and walls and the trail leading out into the night!" cried another thane, standing helplessly with his sword in his hand.

"What monster could have done this?" wondered a third.

A great cry arose from the remaining warriors as they stared, powerless, at the monster's bloodstained tracks, realizing that many of their companions were dead.

The sound of weeping filled the hall. King Hrothgar returned from his sleeping quarters and, gathering his thanes together, heard from them what had happened. The great king sat on his throne, sorrowful and shocked by the news.

The next night the warriors decided to sleep away from the feast hall. But two of Hrothgar's bravest thanes decided to lie in wait on each side of the great door, which was now firmly barred. With their swords drawn, they stood waiting to fight the monster, if he returned.

And Grendel did return. Now that he had tasted the flesh of these noblemen, he wanted more! He crept back silently to Heorot, but this time he found that the door was barred. Grendel's strength was greater than any barred door, and he pushed it open with a single thrust of his powerful hand. His pale eyes swept across the darkness, looking for sleeping warriors.

The two thanes immediately saw Grendel's vile head peering through the doorway, and they sprang up to fight this monster.

"Come!" one cried out. "Now is our chance to find fame!"

Boldly, they swung their swords and ran to slash at Grendel. But even with their great strength and bravery, they were powerless against the monster.

With his claws outspread, the creature grabbed one man in each hand. In a moment he had torn them limb from limb and devoured them.

Night after night other brave men tried to defeat Grendel, but he couldn't be stopped. This nightly terror from the lone monster of the marshlands continued for 12 long years. Neither Hrothgar, the best of kings, nor his Spear-Danes knew what to do. They were in despair.

BEOWULF, THE MAN

In the land of the Geats, years after his famous swim, Beowulf had grown into the mightiest of men. He had proved himself to be a great warrior, and for his bravery King Hygelac had given him a fine hall set in its own land.

One day a group of men traveling in peace across the land of the Geats came to Beowulf's hall looking for shelter. Beowulf's thanes offered them food and drinks, and that evening Beowulf asked their leader for any news that they might have heard during their travels.

"Alas," the leader replied, "our news isn't good. Do you know of the plight that has overcome your neighbors, the Spear-Danes?"

"No," replied Beowulf. "Hrothgar, the king of the Spear-Danes, is a noble man, and I'd be sorry to learn of troubles in that land."

The traveler nodded. "It's a terrible fate for the Spear-Danes. They are being destroyed by a merciless and all-devouring monster known as Grendel." The man went on to tell Beowulf and his listening thanes how the Spear-Danes seemed powerless against this creature.

The Geats listened to the story, and some of the men glanced fearfully around at the black shadows that filled the far corners of Beowulf's hall. Outside, the countryside lay dark and silent. They feared that enemies might be lying there waiting, like Grendel, to destroy them.

"But can none of the Spear-Dane warriors rid their country of this evil?" asked one man.

"It seems that even the bravest of thanes is helpless. Heorot, the great feast hall, becomes a place of terror as soon as the light leaves the sky," replied the traveler.

As Beowulf sat listening to this fearful story, he decided that he must visit King Hrothgar and offer to save the land of the Spear-Danes from Grendel's attacks. The next morning he went to Hygelac, his own king, and told him about his plan.

"With your permission," Beowulf said, "I'll sail to the land of the Spear-Danes and help their great king with his troubles."

Hygelac was afraid that Beowulf, his sister's son, might die in this adventure, but he would not stop the warrior from his brave attempt.

"Beowulf," he replied, "except for my own young sons, you're my closest relative. I fear that if you try to help the Spear-Danes, you too will be killed by this monster Grendel. But I will not stand in your way. If our wise men agree, you may go. To save the old and noble King Hrothgar would be an honorable deed."

The elders of the Geats were called to council. They talked together and decided that fate, which ruled all their destinies, looked kindly on Beowulf. The time to help the Spear-Danes was right.

A ship was prepared, and Beowulf chose 14 of the bravest thanes to go with him. Eagerly, the warriors carried their bright armor to the ship; splendid swords and helmets were placed in the heart of the boat. When everything was ready, Beowulf said goodbye to his king. The men on the shore released the ropes that were holding the great ship. The wind caught its sail and carried the proud vessel, foam-flecked and skimming like a bird, over the ocean that they called the great whale way.

The next morning, as the sun broke through the rain-filled clouds, Beowulf and his men saw the shining headland of the Spear-Danes, wreathed in mists, rising up before them.

On the cliff top a man stood guard as men had been standing guard since before Shield Sheafing's time. The warriors' armor glinted in the sun and caught his eye. He noticed that the armor was ready to be used and wondered whether these men were invaders. He strode down to the beach to meet them, carrying a giant spear in his hand.

He heard a grating sound as the ship pulled onto the sands and saw the first men leap ashore, carrying their gleaming armor. They were powerful men, and the Spear-Dane saw that their leader was the mightiest of them all.

"Halt!" the guard ordered. "Who are you and where have you come from, warriors? Why do you come in a tall ship over the waves to the land of the Spear-Danes? Why do you bring these weapons of war?"

The leader answered. "We've come from the land of the Geats, and we mean no harm."

"Well, I can't let you pass until you tell me why you have sailed to the land of the Spear-Danes," the guard replied firmly. "Tell me at once the reason for your journey!"

Again the leader spoke. "My name is Beowulf. We wish to visit your king, Hrothgar. My father, a noble war-leader, was well known to him, and we come as friends."

The guard lowered his spear. "Welcome, Beowulf and companions. I'll show you the path to King Hrothgar's feast hall," he replied. "But there's little celebration in Heorot these days. Our people suffer greatly."

"We have heard of your king's sorrow and have

come to help. We know Hrothgar to be a wise and good king who's troubled by a creature of terror and evil. We believe that we can rid him of the monster."

The guard gestured to the path winding up the cliff's side. "Come!" he cried. "I'll set some of our men to guard your vessel while you are with King Hrothgar."

Leaving their ship on the shore, the warriors marched to the cliff's top and were led toward the great hall. As they approached Heorot, the most famous building under the skies, the guard stopped.

"I must leave you now, Lord Beowulf. There before you is Heorot. Follow the paved road, and you'll soon reach its great door."

BEOWULF'S BOAST

Beowulf led his warriors in single file along the paved path toward Heorot. The sun flashed on the warriors' bright helmets, and their armor and swords jangled as they marched. When they arrived, in order to show they came in peace, the men laid their broad shields against the building's wall. They set their javelins and spears in a pile against the wall and then sat at ease on the benches outside the main door.

A follower of Hrothgar, standing in the doorway, watched them with sharp eyes. He approached and questioned them.

"Where have you come from, warriors, and why do you bring these weapons of war?"

"I am Beowulf, and these are my companions. We come from the land of the Geats. If you'll take us to your noble lord, King Hrothgar, I'll tell him why we've come," replied Beowulf.

The man bowed.

"I'm King Hrothgar's

messenger. But first I must ask if you've come in peace. Are you a band of men seeking a new chief and do you wish to serve my king?"

There was an angry murmuring among Beowulf's companions at these words.

"We do come in peace, but we are not outlaws forced to find another leader!" cried out one of the men. "We are Geats and serve Hygelac, our own great king!"

The messenger bowed again. "I'll speak to King Hrothgar about your request. Wait here until I return with his answer." He turned quickly into the hall.

King Hrothgar of the Spear-Danes sat at the far end of his great feast hall. His shoulders were stooped, his hair was gray, and there were lines of sorrow on his face.

The messenger strode through the hall and bowed low before his king. "My lord, men from the land of the Geats are waiting outside," he said. "They've journeyed across the ocean, and their leader, whom they call Beowulf, wishes to speak with you. Do not refuse his request, great Hrothgar. Their armor is magnificent, and their chief seems to be a great warrior."

King Hrothgar stirred in his seat, his hands gripping the arms of his chair so that his knuckles showed white. The thanes gathered around him and watched in silence, their faces pale and dejected.

"Beowulf?" he questioned. "Beowulf? I knew him when he was a boy. I also knew his father; he was a good man."

His head dropped, and it seemed like the king's thoughts were lost in the days of old. But after a moment or two, he raised his head.

"It is rumored that Beowulf has the strength of thirty men in the grasp of his hand. Perhaps he's been sent to help us against our foe, Grendel! I'll offer Beowulf and his warriors great riches if they can free us from our torment."

At these words, the thanes in the hall started murmuring excitedly, each one wondering if at last they were to be freed from the nightly terror.

The king's voice rang out again. "Hurry! Ask Beowulf and his companions to come in so that they may see that we, too, have a band of brave warriors and kinsmen around us. Tell them that they are welcome in Heorot, the feast hall of the Spear-Danes. But we must not let them think that we haven't tried to destroy Grendel ourselves."

The messenger returned to the waiting men. "My king asks me to tell you that he knows your leader and welcomes you as bold warriors. Leave your weapons of war outside and enter the hall to speak with Hrothgar."

Beowulf arose with his companions, and they entered Heorot. They strode across the length of the great hall, through the gathered Spear-Danes, who watched silently from their benches. When they stood before Hrothgar, Beowulf called out proudly to the king.

"Greetings, King Hrothgar! I am Beowulf, kinsman of King Hygelac of the Geats. I know about the terror of Grendel. I have heard how Heorot, the greatest of buildings, lies deserted once the brightness is gone from the sky. I've come to fight with the demon, and if fate allows me, I shall free you from this curse!"

A muttering filled the hall, and many of the listening Spear-Danes thought that Beowulf spoke foolishly without understanding.

"Does this visitor think that he

can win so easily where we've failed for so long?" said one man.

"My own brave brother died fighting Grendel," said another, "and he was as powerful as this Beowulf." Beowulf's companions heard these whispers, and one spoke out quickly, stepping up to Hrothgar's seat so that everyone could hear him.

"Do not doubt our leader!" he cried. "The wise men of our land agreed that Beowulf should come to Heorot because they know his strength. They know of the many

battles he's won and of the many terrible creatures, ogres, and water monsters that he's fought and killed!"

Then Beowulf cried out. "Yes, and I will fight alone until the demon, Grendel, is defeated!"

The Spear-Danes were silenced at this boast and sat amazed as Beowulf continued. "Do not refuse my request, noble king! I've come from across the surging seas because I alone may save Heorot. I will not carry a shield or a sword, for I've heard that no weapon made by man can harm Grendel. Instead, I'll grasp the

demon with my bare hands and grapple with him in a fight to the death."

A mighty roar rose up from the hall at these words, but Beowulf held up his hand for silence.

"I don't expect to die and will trust in fate, who knows my destiny. But, should I die, I ask that you return my helmet, sword, and chain mail to my own king."

Hrothgar rose up and stood beside Beowulf. "My friend, we joyfully accept your offer of help. It is with great sorrow that I tell you what the Spear-Danes have endured these past years. Time and again, while seated in this hall, my brave men have laid plans for the destruction of Grendel. They've made promises, even boasts when they've had much to drink. But when night comes, they're unable to win victory over this creature. Their weapons are powerless, and the benches become drenched with blood."

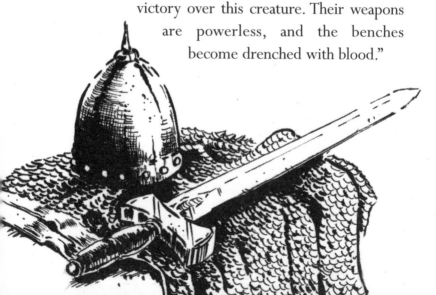

He broke off and clapped his hands.

"But now let us enjoy a feast and talk of daring adventures. We will dream of glory and victory to come!"

A JEALOUS RIVAL

The great feast hall was prepared, and benches were placed for the visitors. A thane filled an ornate cup with mead and carried it around to the seated men. A minstrel sang in a clear voice about the fame of Heorot, and there was great rejoicing among the Spear-Danes and their guests.

But one man alone was filled with angry thoughts. While Beowulf and Hrothgar were speaking, he had remained silent, but his mind was full of bitter jealousy. His name was Unferth. He hated the idea that any man might win greater glory than he. At last, unable to bear his envy any longer, he rose up from his seat of honor near Hrothgar and spoke hostile words.

"Beowulf!" he called out. "Aren't you the man who, in your boyhood, boasted about your own bravery? Didn't you take part in stupid adventures that risked the lives of your companions? Wasn't Breca forced, because of your foolish boast, to risk his life in the surge of the waves? And wasn't he the real victor in your battles with the sea monsters?"

Beowulf's men stirred uneasily and glanced toward their leader, unsure of how they should act after these scornful words.

"Don't think," Unferth continued, "that defeating Grendel will be as easy as your boasting words suggest. I'm sure that even if you dare to wait at night for the monster's coming, your meeting with him will end in disaster."

Beowulf gestured to his men to remain still and turned toward Unferth.

"Well, my friend, I fear that you have drunk too much, and that's why you are speaking in this way."

A wave of laughter ran around the hall at Beowulf's words, and an angry flush stained Unferth's cheeks. But before he could retort, Beowulf continued.

"I know the truth of the adventures of my

youth. Fate spared me and Breca, my companion during many great adventures. Together we defeated nine grim sea monsters, and we both knew that it was I who had the greater strength in those battles. We competed with each other in friendship, and in times of danger we stayed by each other's side."

Beowulf paused and then spoke quietly. "Have you, friend, attempted to slay Grendel? The monster wouldn't have performed so many horrors over these past years if your actions had been as warlike as your words."

At this, Unferth the jealous warrior leaped onto his feet, his own mighty sword drawn and ready in his hand. "Look upon this weapon!" he called out. "This sword is named Hrunting. It is the greatest of all swords. It has never failed yet in any battle!"

Many of the men laughed and asked why, if it was so mighty, he hadn't used his sword against Grendel. Unferth muttered that it was known that no sword could defeat Grendel, but he spoke softly, shamed by these taunts. His sword remained in his hand. Some of Hrothgar's thanes stood up and tried to calm down Unferth.

Beowulf waited until there was silence in the hall, then he spoke again. "The time has come to show Grendel my strength so that Spear-Danes may once more live proudly in their land!"

At these words, some of the Spear-Danes looked at Beowulf with growing hope. The tension was eased further when Wealhtheow, the gracious queen of the Spear-Danes, came into the great hall, accompanied by her ladies. The queen was tall and fair, and her expression was both loving and dignified. She walked proudly, wearing a flowing white dress, finely embroidered in crimson and gold. From her shoulders hung a long cloak with a rich crimson lining and fastened with a golden brooch. Her hair was twisted into bands, and she wore a circle of gold upon her head. In her hands the queen carried a golden goblet studded with gems. She offered it first to her husband Hrothgar. When the king had drunk, the queen turned to the visitors.

"Welcome to our land," she said. She smiled at the Geats, but her eyes were sad. "I've heard that you have come to save my lord and our people from our nightly terror." She held out the golden goblet to Beowulf. "Drink, dear friend, and may your courage be rewarded by success."

Beowulf took the cup and looked at the gracious lady. "When I sailed with my men, I was determined to help your people or die in the attempt. I now make you this promise. I will either slay the monster or meet my end in this hall."

The queen was pleased with his words. "I'll offer thanks to the heavens for sending you to help us in our suffering," she said, taking her seat next to King Hrothgar.

The queen's attendants moved among the nobles and other young men, passing around precious cups of mead. The feasting continued late into the night. The minstrels' music rang through the hall as it had in days gone by. They sang about the Spear-Danes' glorious past and even dared to sing about the glory that they hoped would return.

Then the old king rose. He knew that now that the light was gone, the night stalker Grendel would be planning an attack on Heorot. All of the warriors stood up and saluted each other. Hrothgar embraced Beowulf and wished him victory in the feast hall.

"I've never entrusted Heorot to a stranger before," he said, "but in you I've placed my hope. Keep a careful watch and think of the fame that can be yours."

The king, with his queen and all of the Spear-Danes, left the hall so that only Beowulf and his warriors were left. Beowulf took off his bright armor and gathered his warriors around him.

"I won't fight the monster with sword or spear," he said. "I'll fight him with my strength alone. It won't be easy, but I'll fight the creature hand-to-hand and hope I find glory!"

The warriors, fearful for their leader and thinking that they would never see their own land again, tried to settle themselves down for the night. They planned to stay awake to keep watch with Beowulf, but the mead that they had drunk all evening had been strong. They were soon asleep. Beowulf alone remained awake. His mind was alert as he waited in the dark for the monster Grendel.

FIGHT TO THE DEATH

ut in the dank marshes, Grendel prowled in the darkness. The creature made his way under the rain-filled clouds toward the hall. He knew the path well, and he could see the outline of the building in the dim light. When he reached the entrance, he found that the doors had been fastened with strong iron bars. He laughed silently, knowing his own strength. Effortlessly, he forced the doors open. He stalked into the hall, his eyes gleaming with a dull and ugly light. He saw the rows of sleeping warriors; some lying on benches, others stretched out on the floor with their cloaks wrapped around them.

Grendel gloated at the sight of so many helpless men. He reached out to grasp the closest man. One of Beowulf's beloved thanes was seized and torn apart in a moment. The flesh and bones of the lifeless man became Grendel's first victim that night.

However, when the foul monster reached out toward a second warrior, instead of a sleeping figure, Grendel's scaly fingers met a mighty grasp.

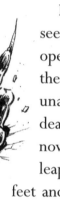

Beowulf had heard and seen the creature force open the door and enter the hall, but he had been unable to prevent the death of his thane. But now he was ready. He leaped silently onto his feet and reached out to grip the monster's hand with the strength of 30 men. Fingers cracked, and bones snapped.

Remembering the promise that he had made earlier that evening, Beowulf stood firm and grappled with Grendel. The monster shrieked, realizing that he had met a power very different to anything that he had fought before. For the first time in his life, Grendel was afraid. He was desperate to escape, to flee back to the mists and swamps that were his home.

Beowulf stepped forward. He tightened his grip on the monster and struggled to overcome him.

"You won't escape from me!" he gasped. "I will not let you destroy the Spear-Danes again!"

The great hall of Heorot echoed with the sounds of the mighty struggle. Beowulf's men, woken by the noise of the fight, leaped onto their feet and gathered around. Some longed to join in with their swords, but they knew that they would do so in vain. The battle between Beowulf and Grendel raged. Sometimes it seemed that Beowulf was about to destroy the monster, but then Grendel, with an angry snarl, would wrestle again with fresh strength. It was a wonder that Heorot's walls didn't collapse as the two fought in a deadly fury. Suddenly Beowulf thrust the monster backward against the benches, which overturned with a deafening crash. But Grendel wasn't defeated yet. In a frenzy of anger he pressed himself upon the warrior. Beowulf, in spite of his great strength, was slowly forced to his knees. Grendel's face, twisted with hatred, looked down at Beowulf as the monster prepared to kill the brave man.

Seeing the danger that their leader was in, the thanes forgot Beowulf's warning that their own swords were of no use against Grendel, and they ran to help. They drew their ancient war swords, but it was just as Beowulf had said. The sharpest blades glanced off Grendel's body; their weapons were powerless against the monster.

As Beowulf fell to his knees, one of his hands still clasped Grendel in its fierce grip. With his other hand, Beowulf grabbed the magnificent spun-gold banners that covered the walls of the hall. He ripped them down, and they fell over the vile creature. For a moment Grendel was confused; he couldn't see his foe, and his strength weakened. Beowulf managed to rise up to his feet as the monster struggled to free himself from the banners.

The watching thanes urged Beowulf on as, once again, the warrior and the demon grappled with each other. The great hall shuddered under the might of the wrestlers as they swayed and struggled for victory. Beowulf's breathing sounded harsh and short, and Grendel, in his terror, gave short screams of pain. Sometimes it seemed that Beowulf would be crushed by Grendel's strength, but just as the men feared that their leader would die, Beowulf would overthrow the demon.

Suddenly a great howl sounded. Beowulf had once again grabbed the scaly hand and was gripping it in a deadly hold. The watching men heard the crack of

more bones as Grendel struggled desperately against this mighty strength. The demon no longer cared about killing anyone or eating human flesh. His only wish was to escape from the terrible grip that threatened his life. He uttered a piercing cry of defeat. He knew that the bones in his hand and arm

had been broken. Then he felt his sinews and flesh tearing, as a gaping wound opened on his shoulder. Grendel's arm had been wrenched from his body!

Freed from Beowulf's grip, the monster turned and staggered out into the blackness of the night. His voice was raised in a shriek of agony as he made his way back to the swamps. A trail of red followed him, and blood gushed from his body. He stumbled blindly along the path until he reached the safety of the vile waters. Grendel knew that his time was over. He plunged into the lake, and his lifeless body sank beneath the foul, bloodstained surface of the water.

A VICTORY FEAST

In Heorot the rejoicing began. Beowulf's companions gathered around the great warrior. They gave thanks for his safety and offered him sweet mead to drink. Beowulf rested on one of the benches, his breath coming in great gasps, as he recovered from his battle.

When morning came, Beowulf took the mighty arm of Grendel and showed it to the Spear-Danes. They were astounded by Beowulf's victory over their ancient enemy.

"Look, Spear-Danes, on your fallen foe!" Beowulf cried. "King Hrothgar, I ask that this arm be nailed high up on the gables of Heorot so that you may long remember this victory!"

As the news of Grendel's defeat spread, men came from far and wide to look at the awesome arm. Still dripping blood, it hung above Heorot's high doors. They stared in astonishment at the sight of the great footprints and the pools of blood leading away from the feast hall's entrance.

The Spear-Danes celebrated that they were now safe after years of misery. Some of the bolder men followed the blood-spattered trail through the

swamps to the lake's banks and stared at the vile redness of the water. Others raced their horses along the wide pathways. A minstrel sang a new song, praising Beowulf for his bold deed.

Then King Hrothgar stood on the steps of Heorot. His queen was with him, and crowds of Spear-Danes were gathered around them.

Hrothgar gazed up at the hideous arm of Grendel.

"Let us give thanks for this sight," he said. "Beowulf, you'll always be cherished by me as my own son. It's certain that your glory will live forever!"

Beowulf bowed to the old king. "I willingly undertook this battle. I had hoped to kill the evil Grendel without further loss of life, but, alas, it was the fate of one of my thanes to die. And I had hoped to kill the monster inside of Heorot so that you could have seen his dead body yourself. But I failed, and the creature managed to break free. But he couldn't have lived long with so terrible a wound."

It was then decided that Heorot must be repaired and redecorated as quickly as possible. Everyone willingly helped and this work. The great broken doors with their shattered bars were fixed. The walls and floor were washed free of blood, and fresh, sweet-smelling rushes were scattered around the hall. The walls were rehung with tapestries embroidered with shining gold. The benches were fixed or replaced with new ones. The torches and fires were relit, and many wonderful treasures, long hidden for fear of the swamp monster, were carried into Heorot for everyone to marvel at. When everything was ready, food and drinks were prepared for a feast. Then Hrothgar stood at the head of the hall.

"Beowulf! Brave companions! You are the most welcome of guests!" he called out loudly. "You will be rewarded well. Fine rings of twisted gold, horses with jeweled saddles, and many ancient heirlooms will be shared among you. And you, Beowulf, will have my own battle armor, which I ask you to take back to your own land."

The noble Hrothgar did not forget the one Geat who had been slaughtered during the night. He gave a bag of gold to Beowulf, asking him to deliver it to the dead man's family.

The rejoicing and happiness at this banquet was greater than ever before, because Beowulf's triumph over Grendel had rescued the Spear-Danes from their long years of misery. Many tales of past glory were retold. Some men, drunk from the mead, boasted about their greatness in the past, and the minstrels sang about brave deeds from long ago.

When the songs were over, Queen Wealhtheow rose. She wore a golden circle on her head and carried a goblet of gold. The lady of the Spear-Danes spoke to Hrothgar in a voice that was soft and sweet.

"Take this goblet, gracious king. Drink to the noble Geats in thanks for what they have done."

She turned to where Beowulf sat with her own two sons and presented to the great warrior a collar of gold and jewels. It was one of the finest pieces ever to be seen, made in earlier times by a race of skilled dwarves.

"Beloved Beowulf, enjoy this ancient treasure that I now give to you with my thanks."

Then the queen returned to her seat, and the warriors celebrated at the banquet. Unferth alone was silent. He made no boasting speeches, and in his heart he knew that Beowulf had spoken the truth earlier.

Late that evening the Spear-Danes led Beowulf and his men to a separate hall, where soft wrappings had been laid ready so that the brave men could rest in comfort. Heorot was once again filled with Hrothgar's own men, sleeping and resting on the benches. That night both the Spear-Danes and the Geats sank into a deep sleep.

How could they know that a second terror awaited them?

GRENDEL'S AVENGER

n a cave deep below the foul water of the lake, an avenger was waiting. Grendel's mother had found her son's dead body, and she brooded over his death. She didn't care about the terror that he had brought to the Spear-Danes over 12 long years. All that she wanted was revenge. She was determined to find and destroy Grendel's slayers.

With great stealth, the she-monster came out of the black water and crawled through the swamps. Her eyes searched for any guard who might see her, but the Spear-Danes no longer kept watch. They were certain that Grendel's death had ended their nightly terror. Grendel's mother moved swiftly through the dark countryside until she saw Heorot in front of her. She approached the great

doors and listened, but no sound came from inside of the hall. The warriors were at peace, sleeping and unafraid. The doors were closed but no longer barred. The creature pushed them open with a single thrust. Eagerly, she seized the Spear-Dane lying closest to the door. She tore the warrior apart and glutted herself on his body, just like her son had done.

The other warriors, awakened by the noise, leaped onto their feet and reached for their swords. But in the dark confusion before anyone could find her, the monster grabbed Grendel's arm and pulled it down from Heorot's gables. Then she turned away and disappeared into the darkness to the stagnant water that was her home.

Great shouting arose from Heorot. Beowulf and his men were

72

in their sleeping quarters, close to the great hall. They were roused by weeping Spear-Danes and told about the new horror that had visited them.

"Beowulf, our king is grieving in Heorot. Please come to him at once!" the Spear-Danes cried.

Beowulf found the old ruler, hunched over on his great throne. His face was like stone. Not only had another demon attacked, but the man who had been killed was Aeschere, one of his councilors—a man of great importance. The Spear-Danes were filled with despair over this new terror.

"Sorrow has come once again to the Spear-Danes!" lamented Hrothgar. "A murderous devil has killed another one of my men, and I don't know who or what it is."

A warrior standing in the midst of the men raised his voice. "I've heard villagers say that there were two creatures, one male and one female, prowling in the wastelands by the foul lake."

Another voice called out. "That's right! And sometimes a mysterious fire is seen leaping on the surface of the water. Few living creatures choose to travel in the wolf-filled hills or to the treacherous marshes close to the lake."

A third voice replied. "This is true. I've heard that stags, running from the hunt, stop at the very edge

73

of the dark water. They won't leap in but prefer to turn and face the hunters rather than swim in the fearful lake."

"Beowulf, once again our salvation depends on you." Hrothgar spoke with despair in his voice. "You haven't seen the place where this second monster has been seen yet, but if you dare to go there, I'll reward you with more treasures."

Beowulf turned to face the Spear-Danes and his own companions. "Come. Let us follow the path to this lake. We Geats cannot return to our own land until we have rescued the Spear-Danes from this new terror. The creature won't escape, not into the center of the earth, not into the forests, not into the depths of the water. I make you this second promise. I will succeed in this deed, too, or die in the attempt!"

THE GIANTS' SWORD

A horse was prepared for the king, and a band of his shield bearers escorted him. Together with Beowulf and his companions, they set off along the track that the monster had taken during the night.

The men moved over the swampy land along a narrow path that led them across mountains, under steep crags, and close to the dens of many unnamed

monsters. At last they reached joyless woods at the edge of a lake. Scum-covered trees, bare of leaves, leaned over slimy rocks at the water's edge. The water of the lake was stagnant, and the men saw with horror that the surface was stained with blood. It was a dreadful place of foul mists and nameless horrors. As they stood at the water's edge, one of the warriors cried out in shock.

"Look!" He pointed toward a marshy piece of land, streaked with blood. "There's Aeschere's head."

The Spear-Danes lifted the head gently and wrapped it in a cloth.

"Aeschere will have a burial worthy of his noble nature," Hrothgar promised.

The warriors looked into the bloodstained water. They saw serpents, strange dragons, and water monsters swimming in the foul water. One of Beowulf's thanes shot an arrow at a coiled serpent as it lay on a rock so that it fell dead into the water. Another thane defiantly sounded his hunting horn. The notes echoed over the desolate water and sent the creatures plunging into the depths. After a minute or two, Beowulf spoke. "Come, it's time for me to seek this second monster and destroy it as I destroyed the first one," he said.

Beowulf's men helped him into his warrior's armor. The hand-woven chain mail, beautifully made, would protect him from all warlike creatures. They placed the great golden helmet on his head, and he stood, ready to leap into the water. But then Unferth, who had spoken no more jealous words, stepped forward.

"Beowulf," he said. "Take my sword, the mighty Hrunting. Its edge is made of iron hardened in battle, and the blade's pattern is soaked in poison. It will serve you well."

Beowulf looked at Unferth. He saw that he regretted the insults that he had made at their first meeting. But he also saw that Unferth was afraid of risking his own life against the monsters in the swirling water. Gravely, Beowulf took the sword and thanked Unferth. He knew that the man was ashamed of his fears and had lost his chance of glory.

Beowulf turned to where the king stood by his horse. "King Hrothgar, I'll fight with this new monster, but if death sweeps me away, take care of my thanes and let them carry my treasures back to our king. Also let Unferth receive my own sword, for I intend to earn glory for myself with his sword, Hrunting, or perish."

With these words, Beowulf stepped forward and leaped into the water of the lake.

Down and down Beowulf swam, thrusting with his strong arms against the stained and icy water. He fearlessly defended himself with the sword, Hrunting, against many creatures that tried to seize him. One unknown monster grabbed him by the leg, but Beowulf struck easily and swiftly, sending the beast to its death in the muddy bottom of the lake. A water serpent tried to strike the warrior with its poisonous fangs, but again Hrunting saved Beowulf from this danger. Through most of that day he braved the cold water. Swarms of vile water creatures pursued him, charging at him with their horns. But Beowulf's chain mail and Unferth's sword saved him from their powers. At last he could see the bottom of the lake.

Close to a lofty cavern an evil monster waited for Beowulf. Grendel's mother sensed the warrior's presence, and she crouched down outside of the cavern. As he came close, she made a grab at his body, clutching at him with her iron-tipped claws. She dragged him toward the cavern's entrance. Once inside, Beowulf saw that the water didn't reach there, and there was no danger from the waves. The place was lit by a pale gleam of light, flickering and cold in a hostile world. In the corners of the cavern, glowing dully, Beowulf glimpsed heaps of treasures that the two monsters had seized from the Spear-Danes over the long years.

Beowulf had no time to look further at these wonders because the demon creature had him in a terrible grip. Again Beowulf's shirt of chain mail protected him from the monster's claws that couldn't pierce through the woven rings. Tearing himself free from the creature's clutches, he stood upright. Wielding the mighty sword, Hrunting, he struck a resounding blow at the monster's head. In that instant he realized that, as with Grendel, no weapon made by man would destroy this second demon. The sword may have been victorious in many battles in the past, and it had saved Beowulf as he swam in the lake, but now it was powerless against the evil of this demon creature. Again and again Beowulf struck, but the sword did not harm the monster.

Still, Beowulf refused to give in. Remembering his battle with Grendel, he threw the sword to one side and grappled closely with the monster. He caught his foe's shoulder in one powerful hand and, with the other, wrestled the creature to the ground. But falling backward, the demon clutched at Beowulf and pulled him to the floor. In a swift move the foul monster twisted to one side and, with desperate strength, pinned the warrior to the ground and pulled out a sharp, bright-edged knife. Beowulf saw the snarling mouth and savage eyes staring down at him and the pointed knife ready to strike. But once again the strong chain mail saved his life—the point of the blade was unable to pierce through the links. Without this help, the mighty warrior would have met his death in the depths of the lake.

Quickly, Beowulf struggled free and leaped onto his feet again. In that moment he saw, hanging on

the wall of the cavern, an ancient sword. It was a mighty weapon, made long ago by a race of giants. It was larger and stronger than any sword that had been made by man. Beowulf, who had the strength of 30 men in his hand grasp, managed to lift the sword off the wall. As he seized the ringed hilt, the monster leaped toward him. Beowulf struck with all his power. Blood sprang along the mighty blade and dripped onto the floor. With one sweep of the sword, Beowulf had struck the monster dead.

BEOWULF'S TROPHY

The pale and flickering light that Beowulf had first seen when he entered the water monster's cavern was changing. There was a new brightness, as if the sun had suddenly appeared. It was time for Beowulf to return to his companions, who had been waiting fearfully at the edge of the lake. But before leaving the dreadful lair, Beowulf wanted to take something that would show the Spear-Danes that their terrors were really over.

Looking around him, Beowulf saw, lying on a blood-soaked bench at the back of the cavern, Grendel's dead body. It was Grendel who had originally brought fear to the Spear-Danes; Grendel who had brought death and terror to all at Heorot. Seeing the monster's head would bring the Spear-Danes relief after years of torment. Beowulf once more gripped the great giants' sword and, with a single blow, cut off the dead creature's head. Fresh blood spewed from the severed head and ran toward the entrance of the cavern. It started to drift upward, mingling with the blood from the other slain monster, out of the cave and up toward the lake's surface.

Beowulf then looked at the treasures heaped around the cavern but decided to leave them where they lay. The only treasure he would take would be the sword that he had seized from the wall—the giants' sword that had helped him to victory.

So, gripping Grendel's hair in one hand and the giants' sword in the other, and with the sword Hrunting sheathed at his side, Beowulf prepared for his journey back up through the water.

Then a strange thing happened. The blade of the sword, the mighty and all-protecting sword forged by giants, began to melt as though it was made of ice. It was as if the blood from the two monsters had been too hot and poisonous for the blade. Beowulf was astounded as the hard metal blade slowly melted away, drop by drop, like an icicle freed from the grip of winter. Soon only the ringed hilt remained, but Beowulf decided to keep it with him. He turned away from the evil place and surged upward to the distant surface. As he swam, he saw the water of the lake becoming calmer and clearer. No vile creatures of the deep attacked him this time. The death of the two monsters had left the lake free of evil.

All through the long hours, on the banks of the lake, Beowulf's thanes, together with Hrothgar and the Spear-Danes, had sat staring at the water. They saw the waves surging with blood.

"Look!" cried one of the Spear-Danes, pointing across the lake. "See the blood swirling in the water. We'll never see Beowulf again!"

"You're right," said another. "The monster has destroyed the great warrior."

"Wait!" called a third. "The blood is clearing. The waves are starting to sparkle! The lake is becoming calm."

The noblemen waited throughout the day, praying that Beowulf would return. They saw the basking water creatures disappear from the rocks and the water become clear and blue. But still there was no sign of Beowulf, and some feared that their protector had been killed in the depths of the lake. Toward evening King Hrothgar rose to his feet.

"I fear that we will never see the valiant Beowulf again," he said sadly. "He has died fighting to help the Spear-Danes. We must return to Heorot, where we will mourn both his and Aeschere's death with honor."

The Spear-Danes left the lake with their king and turned back toward Heorot. But Beowulf's thanes stayed at the water's edge, their minds filled with anxious fear. They were desperate to see their leader again, and they grew more troubled with each passing minute.

Suddenly the surface of the water broke. Sparkling drops rose from the lake, and waves of clear water rolled toward the banks. With a shout, one of the watching Geats rose up and pointed across the lake.

"See where the water is stirring! Something is rising from the lake's depths!" he cried.

The waiting group stared at the water's surface. Then they saw Beowulf swimming toward them, and they hurried to the edge. Beowulf's loyal thanes helped him out of the water. One of them took his great helmet, and others loosened and removed his chain

mail. His followers rejoiced as they gathered around their leader to hear his tale. They stared in wonder at Grendel's huge head and at the mighty sword hilt that Beowulf still grasped.

Then they prepared to retrace their steps across the swamplands and desolate countryside, back to Heorot.

"It'll take the strength of four thanes to carry Grendel's head," Beowulf said. "Who will do it?"

Four of the young men eagerly offered, proud to carry such a trophy back to Heorot. Beowulf himself carried the sword Hrunting and the hilt of the ancient sword made by giants.

When Beowulf and his warriors reached Heorot, they marched through the mighty doors. The floor rang with the sound of their steps as they carried Grendel's head to where Hrothgar and his lady sat. The young men stood proudly before the watching Spear-Danes, who stared in amazement at their defeated enemy's terrible head.

Beowulf raised his hand. "Greetings, Hrothgar, king of the Spear-Danes. See where your enemy lies dead. And the second monster is also slain."

Hrothgar's eyes were filled with tears as he looked upon the great warrior. "I thought that I'd never see you again," he said in a low voice.

"Fate was on my side. It wasn't my destiny to die in that lake," Beowulf replied. "My battle under the water wasn't easy, but I was determined to win. Look at these trophies that we have brought you as a sign of my success."

He turned to Unferth, who stood at the edge of the crowd. "My thanks, Unferth," he said nobly. "Hrunting is a fine and victorious sword that helped me against the monsters in the lake." Not by one word did Beowulf blame the sword for failing him in his last battle.

Then Beowulf continued telling of his adventures, of how he fought his way down to the monsters' cavern, of his battles with the evil lake dwellers, and of his final battle with the second water demon, Grendel's mother.

"Just in time, I saw hanging upon the wall of the cavern an ancient and beautiful sword made by giants of long ago. With it, I was able to slay the monster."

Beowulf raised aloft the hilt of the sword. A murmur ran around the watching men, and they craned forward to see what it was that Beowulf held.

"But after my struggles, the mighty blade of this sword melted away from the poison of the two monsters. See how only the hilt remains. Hrothgar, your enemies are dead, and you may now live and sleep in Heorot, free from nightly fear. All your followers, trusty warriors, and eager youths may rejoice that the Spear-Danes are saved!"

The great hilt, gleaming and decorated, was handed to Hrothgar, the old war leader. For a long while he stared at the hilt, examining it, then he spoke slowly.

"Look where the hilt is engraved in ancient runes! It tells the story of the flood and how mankind was saved from the surging water."

The noble king looked at Beowulf. "Your triumph, Beowulf, will always be remembered by my people." Hrothgar's voice cracked as he continued, "Every nation will honor you. And I know that you will live long to comfort your own people."

Then Hrothgar rose up, lifted a goblet, and spoke to all of the gathered men. "Let us now join in the joy of the feast. In the morning I'll distribute fine treasures among you."

Once again a great banquet was spread, and the warriors celebrated until the black cover of night spread over Heorot. Finally, the gray-haired king left the hall. Beowulf, exhausted from his adventures, slept in Heorot, while over him the great roof, arched and decorated with gold, towered into the night sky.

THE JOURNEY HOME

The next morning, with the sun's brightness filling the world with light, Beowulf and his thanes were eager to get back to their ship. They longed to sail back to their homeland to tell of their adventures.

Beowulf approached the throne where Hrothgar was seated. "My thanks, King Hrothgar, for the kindness that you've shown us. If ever news should reach us again that the Spear-Danes are in danger, we'll gladly help you. I know my own king, Hygelac, would allow me to bring a thousand thanes with spears and swords to your aid!"

"You are a brave and wise man," Hrothgar replied. "Should the time come when your own country, the land of the Geats, needs to choose a king, then they could choose no one better than you."

With those words, the king brought out great treasures, which he gave to the heroes. "Dear Beowulf, take this bright coat of chain mail, this great helmet, and sword. They've belonged to the kings of the Spear-Danes for centuries, but it's now right that you should take them. Offer them to your own king!" As he clasped Beowulf to him, tears fell from the old man's eyes. "I will never forget what you have done for us. Our two countries will now always live in friendship!" he cried.

Beowulf and his warriors marched from Heorot, back

to where their ship awaited them. The guard on the cliff top saw Beowulf and his men approaching and came to greet them.

"You'll always be welcome in the land of the Spear-Danes," he said.

Then the curve-necked ship was loaded with the treasures—fine battle armor, horses with jeweled saddles, twisted rings and collars of gold, and decorated swords. Before they sailed, Beowulf thanked the watchman for keeping their ship safe and presented him with a gold-hilted sword as a reward.

Beowulf's thanes pushed the ship out to sea and clambered on board. The sail was unfurled and a

gentle wind filled it. The timbers of the ship creaked and groaned as the waves carried it on its journey over the ocean's currents, following the great whale way to the land of the Geats. The figure of the watching guard grew faint and finally disappeared as the ship sped over the sea.

The journey home was without incident. No monsters from the deep troubled the Geats, and the wind was kind to them so they made good progress. As they spied the cliffs of their own land in the distance, Beowulf and his companions whooped with joy. Carried by the wind and tides, the ship swept forward until it rested firmly on the sands. The harbor guard, who had been watching anxiously for the warriors, hurried to the water's edge and helped tie up the vessel. "Welcome home, Lord Beowulf!" he cried. "We've been watching the sea, waiting for your return."

Then Beowulf called out to his companions. "Take the treasures from our ship and carry them to King Hygelac!" The thanes gathered together all of the rich treasures and set off toward the king's dwelling, close to the sea wall. In the sky the sun shone warmly from the south as Beowulf and his men marched briskly. At the entrance to King Hygelac's great hall a gathering of his men called out excitedly as the returning warriors strode through the doorway. Hygelac was seated at one end of the hall with his queen, Hygd. He sprang onto his feet and greeted Beowulf warmly, while his men hurried to fill the goblets with mead. Then Hygd, the wise and gentle queen, carried a jeweled cup among the gathered people.

"Beloved Beowulf," Hygelac said. "I long to hear about your adventures. When you left us so suddenly, I feared that I'd never see you again. Although I admired you for your brave action, I feared that you might be going to your death. I've often thought about you, and now I thank God that you've returned safely."

Beowulf told about the adventures that he'd had

and how he had destroyed Grendel and the second monster. The listening men loved hearing about these great battles. Beowulf also spoke about the treasures that Hrothgar had given them as a reward.

"You, noble Hygelac, are my closest relative, and therefore a great part of these treasures must be yours."

The thanes led the magnificent horses forward and laid before their king the golden ornaments and other treasures. As for the ancient battle armor of the Spear-Danes, Beowulf presented this to King Hygelac as Hrothgar had instructed.

Finally, Beowulf held up the fine gold collar, made by dwarves in earlier times, that Hrothgar's queen had given to him. "I wish to give this collar to our queen. This necklace, made of twisted gold and encrusted with gems, was given to me by Hrothgar's queen, and I offer it now to Hygelac's queen." Queen Hygd accepted the generous gift, saying it was the most beautiful jewelry that she had ever seen.

To honor Beowulf, Hygelac ordered that the ancient sword of the Geats be brought in. Taking it in his hands, the king rose up and stood before Beowulf.

"Beowulf, take this heirloom of our people. It's right that it should be yours!" And Hygelac laid the sword in Beowulf's lap.

A great shout rose up from the watching Geats,

and they celebrated late into the night. They rejoiced that Beowulf had won such glory for his people. Beowulf and his thanes rejoiced that they were back in their own homeland, the land of the Geats.

DEATH OF A KING

The years passed, and Beowulf continued to act with bravery and honor in his homeland, the land of the Geats. Hygelac, his king, rewarded him with treasures and land and a high position in the kingdom.

But war was never far away.

One day King Hygelac called Beowulf to his great hall. "Beowulf," he said, "I have been thinking that it's time we Geats won ourselves more treasures and honor. We can do this in a battle if we are victorious. What do you say?"

Beowulf didn't want to attack anyone while the

Geats were living in peace, but Hygelac was determined to seek further treasures from among the neighboring tribes.

Queen Hygd, like Beowulf, was worried about her husband's decision. "Beloved Hygelac," she said, "I do not like your plans to go to war against our neighbors. However, if fate has decided, let it be so. Take my necklace, which was made long ago by skilled dwarves. You will remember that Beowulf gave it to me when he returned from the land of the Spear-Danes. Wear it in battle, and may it grant you victory and keep you safe!"

Hygelac assembled a mighty army. His men sailed up the river in huge warships to the land of the Franks, whose country bordered the river. There, they ruthlessly ravaged the land, burning everything in their way. They plundered and looted mounds of treasures from the helpless Franks.

But all was not well. As the victorious Geats were returning to their ships, disaster struck. The king and Beowulf were among a troop of Geats who, thinking that the Franks had been defeated, decided to rest before boarding their ships. Without warning, a group of Franks attacked in a final attempt to win back their treasures. Beowulf's sharp ears heard the crack of twigs underfoot and the rustle of men

pushing through undergrowth. He sprang to his feet
and shouted a warning.

"Hygelac!" he called. "Look out! Enemies behind!"

The Geats prepared for battle as the horde of
Franks rushed forward from their hiding place.
Men grappled with each other. Some slashed savagely
with their great swords, others stabbed with
daggers. Blood soon spilled on the grass, already
churned into mud from the many feet
trampling on it. Terrible cries ripped
the air as the two forces battled
fiercely.

A trumpeter rose to sound his horn in an attempt to summon help from the main party of Geats, but he was instantly struck down by a powerful blow from an enemy sword.

Beowulf, seeing Hygelac trapped

in the middle of a savage group of Franks, forced his way toward his leader. Hygelac was fighting bravely, but his enemies outnumbered him. They knew that he was the king, and this made them determined to kill him on the battlefield.

"Hold fast!" Beowulf called out as he wielded his sword, cutting and slashing his way through the men.

But it was no use. Just as Beowulf reached the ring of men surrounding the king, he saw one of the Frankish warriors raise his sword above Hygelac's head.

"Hygelac!" Beowulf shouted, but even as he spoke, he saw the sword crash down on the king's helmet. Hygelac fell, his helmet splitting in two. He was mortally wounded; nothing could save him now. As his body lurched forward, Hygelac's eyes stared across at Beowulf. The two men, king and lord, kinsmen and friends, looked into the other's faces. Hygelac tried to speak, tried to let Beowulf know about the love he had for him. Beowulf, too, tried to call out words of encouragement to his king. But neither could do more than look at the other before Hygelac's life slipped away. His body fell to the ground. The precious collar of twisted gold, rich with jewels, broke loose. It was smeared with the king's blood and lay trampled into the mud. It had brought him no luck.

Seeing his king die, Beowulf felt great pain. He wished that Hygelac had never set out on this fatal war. He wished that he could have persuaded him not to seek more treasures. Hygelac's death on the battlefield filled Beowulf with sorrow and anger.

Before him, he saw the standard bearer of the Franks, laughing in triumph at the death of the Geat king. In an instant, Beowulf threw his sword to one side and sprang toward the man. His mighty hands, which held the strength of 30 men, tightened themselves around the enemy's neck.

Tearing aside the protective armor, Beowulf's hands pressed upon the terrified man. Although the Frank struggled to escape from the tightening hold, he was unable to save himself and slowly sank to the ground as his life ended. Seeing the standard bearer dead and the standard lying trampled in the mud, Beowulf bent over the fallen man and picked up the sword that lay beside him. He recognized the sword as the famous Naegling, a sword forged in earlier times. With Naegling in his mighty hand, Beowulf strove to defeat the Franks single-handedly. He

succeeded in striking down many of these warriors, but one by one his own men, too, were killed around him.

Beowulf saw his thanes bleeding on the ground where they had fallen. Desperately, he tried to rally the remaining men, but it wasn't their destiny to survive this battle. They, like their king, lay dead, and Beowulf was alone.

KING BEOWULF

eowulf knew that, in order to escape, he needed to reach one of the Geats' ships before they sailed. He collected armor from his dead companions, and, carrying this load, he made his way toward the riverbank.

As he battled through the undergrowth, he had to keep a careful watch out for Franks who were searching the countryside for any Geats who had escaped from the battle. Three times Beowulf had to lie crouched behind bushes as bands of the enemy went past. But three times fate must have been on his side, for although many eyes looked for him, none saw him. Beowulf longed to leap out from his hiding places and slay more of the enemy, but he knew that to do this would mean certain death. It took him many hours to reach the river where the ships had been moored. As he got close to the river, to his horror he saw large numbers of Geats lying dead in the undergrowth.

Beowulf looked down at his dead comrades. In spite of their initial victory, the Geats had been defeated by the savage Franks. Beowulf knew that he must return home and tell the story of the battle; how the Geats had won victory and treasures at first, but then how Hygelac had been slain and the treasures and final battle had been lost.

Beowulf stood on the bank of the great river, gazing toward his own land. There was no sign of the ships, and he feared that the Franks had destroyed them. He also knew that he couldn't sail a warship single-handedly through the dangerous water. How was he to cross the mighty river? Then he remembered the adventures of his youth. He recalled how he and his friend Breca had swum for seven days and seven nights in the ocean.

Today I'll repeat that bold adventure, he thought. *If I could battle with the waves then, I can do it again today!* He strapped the armor of 30 men onto his back and arms, and, without wasting any more time, waded into the cold water.

Beowulf fought with the river and its currents for many hours. Having escaped from the Franks, he would not be defeated by the water. Slowly, he made his way from one bank toward the other. There were no monsters to fight, just strong and angry currents. He did not want to be swept downstream to the sea or pulled underwater to lie trapped in the weeds. At last, Beowulf felt firm land beneath his feet. He staggered onto the bank and lay there for a moment to regain his strength. He was wet, cold, and exhausted, but he turned his face toward the sun and was glad to feel its warmth upon him.

Then he stood up and trudged slowly toward his

home. Sentries saw the lone warrior and ran to help him. Beowulf went straight to Hygd, the wife of the slain King Hygelac, and told the queen of her husband's brave death fighting the Franks. The news of their king's death spread throughout the land of the Geats, and the people mourned. His death made them fearful for their future. Hygelac's eldest son, Heardred, was only a boy. Neighboring tribes might try to conquer the Geats while their new king was still so young.

Queen Hygd was still sorrowful about her husband's unnecessary death. Now she also feared that her son was too young to be a king and rule wisely. She called the people together and, before them, turned to Beowulf.

"Beloved Beowulf," she said. "We are all grieving over the death of our king, my dear Hygelac, and of so many brave warriors. But we must also think about the future. My son, Heardred, is still too young to carry the burdens of a king. Therefore, before our gathered people, I offer you the throne. You have proved that you are wise and brave. You will guide our nation safely over the coming years."

A shout rose up from the people. They, too, felt that Beowulf would be a good and strong king.

But Beowulf shook his head. "I cannot take the place of our prince, my young kinsman," he said. "The throne is his by right as it was his father's before him."

Those listening spoke among themselves, some saying that Beowulf's words were true, but others fearing what might happen to the land of the Geats if Beowulf didn't become their king.

Finally, one of the elders stepped forward, and the others fell silent. "Beowulf speaks well!" he cried. "Let the young prince be our king, but let Beowulf be his guide."

For a few years the Geats lived in peace. Their young king, Heardred, was good and fair, guided wisely by Beowulf. But fate was not kind, and soon another war broke out. This time the Geats were attacked by the Swedes. In the clash of the battle the young king was struck down by the stroke of a mighty sword.

When the war was over, once again the people gathered together to find a way through their troubles, and again an elder finally spoke out.

"It was not long ago that Hygelac's heir, the young prince, became our king. He was worthy of his heritage, but before he could prove his strength, he has been taken from us in battle."

The gathered men murmured among themselves, and some turned their eyes toward Beowulf, where he sat close to the empty throne.

"Now we must choose again," the man continued. "At our last gathering some of us offered the throne to Beowulf, but he rightly refused it. Now Heardred is gone. Beowulf, again we ask you to be our king for as long as you're granted life. It is the wish of the Geats." Silence fell over the hall, and every man watched Beowulf. Slowly, he rose to his feet and spoke.

"You are right. We must look to the future. Heardred, our king, is slain, and I will accept what you are offering me. I will rule the people of the Geats with care and strength as long as I can."

A great cheer rose into the rafters of the hall at Beowulf's words. Beowulf, the mighty warrior, was king!

THE TREASURE HOARD

For 50 winters Beowulf ruled the kingdom of the Geats. He was a wise protector of his people, and he was honored by the nation. Then terror struck in the land of the Geats, and, although Beowulf was now an old man, the great adventures of his youth had not been forgotten. It was to their king that the people turned for help.

Many centuries before, a noble and ancient tribe of people had collected a vast treasure of gold and jewels. With the passing of the years, this ancient tribe was carried away by war and famine until only one survivor remained. This lone man gathered together all of the treasures and placed them inside of a barrow—a huge earth mound built by giants on a cliff edge looking out over the great ocean. After this man's death, no one remembered about the hidden treasures.

One night a fiery dragon discovered the secret passage that led into the center of the mound. The dragon followed

the passage into the heart of the barrow and saw something glittering inside. Great heaps of twisted gold, golden plates and wine cups, goblets and flagons, jewels of every color, necklaces, collars and rings, and ornate swords and helmets lay heaped inside of the mound. And no human knew that it was hidden there!

The dragon stared at the treasures, unable to believe its eyes. It had never seen such a sight before and was determined to keep everything for itself. This fiery sky serpent made its home inside of the barrow, and for 300 years it kept watch over the hoard.

One winter's evening during Beowulf's reign, a slave, escaping from his master, ran desperately across the cliff, looking for a place of safety. This man knew nothing about the dragon's hoard, but he needed somewhere to hide. Stumbling by chance upon the opening of the passage, he ran inside, hoping to escape from the men who were chasing him.

Exhausted, he slumped against the side of the tunnel. He looked back in terror at the way he had run, but there was no sign of his pursuers. After a minute or two his breath, which had been coming in great gasps, slowly quieted. He stood up and looked around fearfully. A new terror gripped him as he saw great stone arches opening up beyond the entrance of the barrow.

"What ancient tribe made these great works?" he wondered. "Could it have been giants? And who now uses this hidden place as a home?"

The man didn't know whether to return to the outside world, where perhaps men were still searching for him, or stay in this place that might shelter unknown enemies. He decided to explore a little farther down the tunnel and crept silently along the passageway. Tense and afraid, he arrived in the heart of a cavern. He didn't know of the sleeping terror guarding the treasures. He couldn't see the fiery serpent who was about to strike.

"Ruler of the heavens, protect me!" he breathed, scarcely believing what he saw in front of him.

Only the faintest light gleamed in the cave, but it was reflected in a thousand glittering points. The secret hoard gave off sparkling, winking lights of every color. Across this heap of magnificent treasures sprawled an enormous, scaly, sleeping dragon. Its head faced the watching man, and its tail lay in massive coils over the piles of gold. The sight of this sleeping monster drove all thoughts of treasures out of the man's mind. At first he wanted to run from this place of certain death before he was seen by the

terrible guardian of the riches. Quietly, he started to turn away to return through the tunnel to the outside world again.

Better to take my chances against men of my own race, he thought, *than to challenge a creature such as this dragon.*

Then an idea came into his mind. *If I could take just one of these magnificent golden vessels,* he thought, *I could offer it to my lord to buy my freedom. I'm sure that he would willingly accept so rich a gift in exchange for one poor slave's life. Then I could live as a free man among my own people.*

He stared around the cave furtively, looking for a fine piece of ancient treasure. His eyes fell on a great jeweled goblet lying on its side, close to the dragon's head. With stealthy footsteps, the slave crept across the floor of the chamber, scarcely daring to breath. Silently, his hand stretched out toward the goblet, and he gently eased it away from the dragon. But no matter how careful he was, the golden goblet clinked against other vessels, and some pieces of jewelry jingled as they shifted slightly in the pile. The man paused and looked quickly at the sleeping monster. Miraculously, it still didn't stir. He held his breath as the goblet finally came free from its resting place, and he clutched it to his chest. Then, wasting no time, he tiptoed back through the great arches into the passage and hurried soundlessly away.

Outside of the mound there was no sign of the men who had been searching for him, and the slave reached his lord's hall without being stopped. There, before his master, he threw himself on his knees and begged for mercy.

"See, my master, this golden vessel. I've wrestled this from a dragon's hoard and now offer it to you in exchange for my freedom."

The lord took the goblet from his trembling slave. Slowly, he turned it in his hands and looked with great surprise at the rich carvings on its sides, set with many jewels. The vessel was more magnificent then anything he had among his own treasures.

"A dragon's hoard?" he said. "Where did you find this dragon's hoard?" The lord looked keenly at the man kneeling before him. "And how is it that you weren't killed by the dragon?"

"Master, the dragon lay asleep. It was stretched across a giant heap of treasures and jewels, but I managed to escape from its cave with this one vessel."

"A heap of treasures? Are these treasures still there?"

The slave nodded. He was eager for his freedom, but he feared that his master would demand to be taken to the dragon's mound and shown its secret entrance.

"Well, I'll grant you your freedom for bringing me this golden goblet," the lord said, "but I'll want you to lead me and a troop of my men to this mound so that we may collect the remaining hoard. Go now! I'll call for you again when I've had time to consult my thanes and have decided on what action I'll take to defeat this dragon."

So just as he had planned, the slave gained his freedom. But before his master could even attempt to gather the dragon's hoard, terror and destruction came to the Geats.

THE DRAGON'S
VENGEANCE

When the dragon awoke, it knew at once that the treasures had been disturbed and that a piece was missing. It was swollen with rage. It alone was the guardian of the hoard—every golden vessel and every gleaming jewel! The dragon was determined to find the person who had dared to take away any part of the treasure. It saw tracks in the dirt and went sniffling along the ground, searching for the scent of the thief.

Spewing out fiery breaths, the dragon hunted back and forth inside of the barrow. It followed the man's tracks in the dust and searched in every corner for a hiding place, but without success. Then it crawled outside, hunting again and again around the great mound. It sniffed at the air and sniffled on the cold ground for any sign of the thief. When it had looked around the outside of the barrow and found neither thief nor treasure, it rose up heavily into the still air. The dragon's huge body was lifted up into the sky by its giant wings. It began to circle slowly in the sky, peering down at the countryside that lay below. Around and around it flew, circling in vain, trying to discover where the thief had escaped to. The dragon

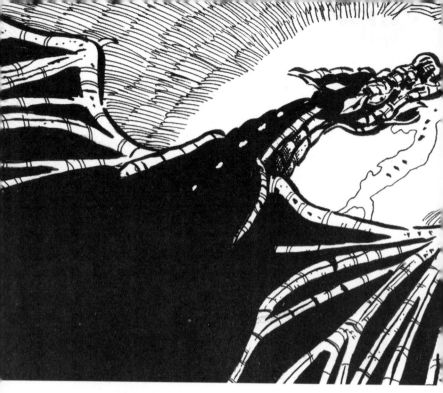

could hardly control its anger. Its wicked nature preferred darkness, so it decided to wait until nightfall before flying again in the black sky. It would then bring vicious revenge to the people nearby.

The hours of daylight passed slowly, but at last the flying serpent was able to carry out its evil wish. It left the great treasure mound and, throwing out great tongues of fire, rose up into the night sky.

Below, it could see a few lights shining from the fires of the Geats, but most of the countryside was covered in darkness as the people slept. The dragon was determined to bring disaster to the innocent

Geats, so it began a night of dreadful torment. From its wide jaws, great spouts of burning flames shot out, setting fire to the wooden houses below. The flames devoured buildings in great bursts of heat. People ran, screaming into the night, but there was no place to escape to. The Geats' villages were encircled with dreadful fire, bringing terror to everyone and death to many. As a new day gradually dawned, the sky serpent's power diminished, and the raging fires died down. The dragon swiftly returned to its treasures inside of the barrow, feeling triumphant at what it had done.

The surviving Geats looked in dismay at what had happened. Women clutched their crying children and stared at the wrecks of their homes. Men wandered among the smoldering remains, feeling powerless against such fury. The land had been destroyed from the coast to far inland. Then news came that not only had many houses and villages been burned, but the great hall of Beowulf, king of the Geats, had been caught in the flames.

Concerned about the fate of their king, men hurried to the destroyed hall. Black, smoking stumps of wood pierced the morning sky, and nothing remained of the proud building. However, the Geats' relief was great when they discovered that Beowulf had escaped with his life.

"If our great king still lives," one said to another, "we'll rebuild our villages and our homes."

"Yes," agreed another. "Beowulf will know how to overcome this disaster."

At first Beowulf was very worried. He was afraid that he had angered the ruler of the heavens in some way. He sat on a rock close to his destroyed hall and stared at the twisted, black timbers. His mind was filled with dark thoughts.

"What ancient law have I broken?" he asked his warriors. "Am I to blame for this disaster? What have I done to bring this trouble to my people?"

A young thane, who was now one of Beowulf's companions, spoke out. He was Beowulf's cousin, and his name was Wiglaf. "This is no punishment for any act of yours!" proclaimed Wiglaf. "It's the act of an evil sky serpent. We must find the creature and destroy it before it can bring further horror to us."

When Beowulf heard Wiglaf speak, he knew that he, the king, must save his people. It was no use wasting time with melancholy thoughts. That wouldn't help the Geats.

Beowulf rose up and stood before his companions. "Wiglaf speaks well," he said. "I'll bring revenge on the sky serpent who has done this terrible thing to my people!"

Beowulf knew that it would be useless to attack the dragon with a troop of his thanes protected only by their shields. Although the shields were decorated with curving metal patterns, they were made from the wood of lime trees. Wood would be powerless against fire. Instead, Beowulf commanded that a mighty battle shield be made entirely out of iron.

Remembering his battle with Grendel, Beowulf decided that he would not allow any of his thanes to join him in his fight with the dragon but that he would attack the creature alone. Wiglaf and many of his other companions tried hard to make Beowulf change his mind.

"We've fought with you in many battles," they said. "Don't force us to stand aside when you fight the dragon."

But Beowulf wouldn't give way. He wasn't afraid of the battle that lay ahead. Hadn't he fought with many evil monsters in the past? Hadn't he saved Heorot, the great feast hall of the Spear-Danes, from the wickedness of Grendel and the other monster? He was older now, but he was still strong. He was determined to save his own people, the Geats, from this fiery dragon and its flames.

BEOWULF FIGHTS THE DRAGON

Beowulf had heard about the escaped slave's adventure with the dragon and sent for the man who had caused this terrible fate to befall the Geats.

"Now that you're a free man, you may choose your own way of living," said Beowulf. "But as your king, I ask you this one favor. Lead us to the dragon's mound. Show us the secret entrance so that we may find the dragon who guards the treasures."

Although he had won his freedom, the man had been very troubled when he saw how many homes and lives had been destroyed by the angry dragon. Although he was still afraid of the fiery creature's wrath, he knew that he must do what the king asked.

"If I can help in some way to lessen the troubles that I've brought upon the Geats, I'll do so," he said, bowing to his king.

Beowulf gathered 11 of his thanes so that they could help him find the dragon's lair. They prepared themselves with shields and swords. Beowulf carried the great iron shield that had just been forged for him.

The band of warriors approached the barrow where it stood on the cliff above the surging waves.

Inside of this earth mound lay the treasures. Crouched beside this was the ancient guardian, the monstrous dragon, waiting to attack any man who dared to approach. Beowulf's brave companions knew that it wouldn't be easy to defeat this creature or to win the treasures.

The former slave pointed to the hidden entrance. "That is the way," he said. "That's where I ran in my panic. It's through that entrance that you'll find the treasures and the guardian."

Beowulf stopped and sat down close to the cliff's edge. The noble lord gazed out across the ocean, the great whale way where he had swum so often in his youth. He wasn't afraid of the coming fight, but he felt a deep sadness in his heart, and his spirit was restless. He knew that his time on earth was coming to an end and the sorrow that he felt was at the prospect of leaving his homeland.

"I've survived many adventures and fought many battles in my youth," he said to his companions. "I've enjoyed great friendship and feasting. As long as life is granted to me, I will fight for my people. But time is passing, and I feel that music and laughter are for others to enjoy now."

"If I could fight this great terror with my bare hands as I fought with Grendel so many years ago, I would," he said. "However, I know that this vile monster will attack with hot, furious flames. I must therefore protect myself with the finest armor and my new shield of iron."

The mighty king raised himself from the ground. He stood upright before his followers as they put his armor on him and handed him his sword and shield.

Beowulf raised his sword, the ancient Naegling, and spoke. "I won this weapon long ago in a mighty battle when our noble king, Hygelac, was killed. It has served me well over the years. Today I'll trust this sword to help me against the fire serpent. I am now ready in body and spirit to meet my enemy here at the entrance to the barrow."

He spoke to Wiglaf. "Go with the warriors and stand on the mound so that you can see whether I win or the dragon wins. This isn't your fight but mine. Many years ago in the land of the Spear-Danes I promised first to rid them of the monster Grendel and then to save them from the second vicious monster. Those promises I kept. Now I make a third promise, and this time it is to you. I will either win victory over the dragon, or I will perish here!"

Beowulf stood with his great iron shield and watched the thanes, anxious for their king, take their position on the grassy slopes. Some wanted to disobey his orders and stay close, but Wiglaf told them to do as Beowulf had commanded.

When all of the men were standing on the barrow, Beowulf approached the passageway. Beyond the entrance he saw great arches roughly hewn out of the rock, just as the slave had described. But now, through these arches, there gushed a stream of fire, alive and hissing with tongues of flames. Beowulf knew that the dragon was awake. He knew that he could not enter the mound because of this deadly fire. So, instead of marching along the burning passage, Beowulf raised his head and uttered a great war cry, which rang through the silent air and echoed within the mound of earth.

His thanes, standing in safety on the mound, felt a shiver of fear when they heard the cry and wondered what the dragon would do after hearing Beowulf's challenge.

The waiting dragon, crouched deep within the mound, turned its head at the sound. It recognized the cry of a man and felt new hatred in its heart. First it gave out another great blast of scorching heat. The ground hissed as the flames spread over it. Standing at the entrance, Beowulf felt the hot breath and swung up his iron shield to protect himself. He then raised his sword and waited silently to meet the dragon.

Inside of the barrow the dragon prepared for battle. It unwound itself from the coils in which it lay and came sniffling and crawling along the passage. It was filled with venom for the man who was standing boldly at the entrance to the mound, disturbing its peace.

As the monstrous creature reached the entrance that opened out onto the headland, Beowulf swung the ancient heirloom, the mighty Naegling, and struck at the dragon's fearsome head. This blow hit the monster powerfully, but it wasn't strong enough to stop the dragon's attack. The famous sword failed Beowulf and seemed powerless against

the fury of the fire. The murderous flames from
the dragon's mouth flew hot and burning toward
Beowulf.

BEOWULF ALONE

The sheet of flame raced past Beowulf at the entrance to the mound and leaped up the sides, toward his watching companions. The thanes, noble sons of princes, saw their leader surrounded by flames and shielded themselves against the fierce heat. They had never seen such flames before, and in spite of their earlier words, they made no move to help their king. Instead, when the first man turned to flee from the roaring flames, they all turned and ran toward nearby woods to save their own lives.

Beowulf was encircled by flames. Only his iron shield and his sword Naegling could help save him from destruction. But not everyone had fled. Wiglaf, the prince and much-loved kinsman of Beowulf, saw his leader trapped in the fire. He saw the suffering in Beowulf's face, staring out from under the protection of his helmet. Wiglaf was furious when he realized that the other thanes had deserted their king. He knew that he couldn't leave his leader as the others had done.

He shouted out to his companions, "Remember the times we've drunk mead together in our great hall? Remember how our king, Beowulf, gave us all treasures? Remember our boasting words and how we promised to repay our lord in a battle when he needed us?"

But it was useless. The deserting warriors didn't listen to Wiglaf's words. Instead, they took cover in the woods, away from the fiery barrow.

Again Wiglaf raised his voice. "We must help our lord in this terrible fire. It's not right that we should carry home our shields unused. We must defend the life of our king!"

Still the frightened warriors ignored Wiglaf's words. So, grasping his own sword and wooden shield, Wiglaf turned toward the fury of the dragon. He ran through the smoke toward the deadly flames and called out to Beowulf.

"Beowulf, you must defend your life with all your strength! I am here and will help you!"

Hearing Wiglaf's voice, the angry dragon, glowing with terrible flames, advanced a second time. The fire surged forward in waves of heat, burning up Wiglaf's wooden shield. The bold thane moved quickly to shelter behind

Beowulf's shield of iron. At that moment Beowulf, protected by his shield, struck a second blow at the great dragon. This time, as the sword reached its target, Naegling broke; the old and ancient sword had fought its final battle and lost.

A third time the fearsome dragon rushed forward and, with its jaws, grabbed the old and noble warrior in its vicious grip. Beowulf felt his lifeblood streaming from his wounds. He could not protect himself against those terrible jaws. Without thinking about his own safety, Wiglaf rushed to save his king. He was no longer afraid of the flames. With his own great sword, he struck at the dragon's body. This stroke sank deeply into the creature's flesh, and the heat of its fire grew weaker.

Beowulf felt the burning flames begin to fade. He managed to free himself from the dragon's hostile grip and drew a second weapon—a deadly knife— that he carried in his armor. Together, Beowulf and Wiglaf struck at the loathsome creature again and again. Finally, Beowulf struck the fatal blow and slew the mighty dragon.

The flames and smoke died away; the scorching heat lessened. The monstrous serpent of the sky lay dead in the entrance to the mound. Beowulf and Wiglaf were triumphant. They had slain the dragon— the vicious enemy of the Geats.

BEOWULF'S DEATH

Despite his iron shield, Beowulf had been badly burned by the flames. But it wasn't just the fire that had wounded him. A deadly poison from inside of the dragon was seeping into his blood. Barely able to stand, Beowulf felt a searing pain flow through his veins. He knew that he was dying. The noble old warrior staggered to the edge of the cliff and fell to the ground. Wiglaf followed him, scarcely caring about his own wounds. He eased the great helmet from the old warrior's head. Then he gently wiped the blood and grime from his face.

Beowulf spoke. "I have ruled this nation for fifty winters, and in that time no neighboring people have had victory over us in a battle. I've had no angry uprising from my own people, and of this I am proud. I wish that fate had granted me a son, for then I would give my war armor to him. But you, dear Wiglaf, are my closest relation and my heir. The mighty sword, Naegling, failed me in my final battle, but my coat of chain mail served me well. Therefore, I leave you this precious coat and my helmet, engraved with a boar's head. May they serve you as they've served me."

Wiglaf felt great sorrow at these words. He struggled to speak, to find the words to let Beowulf know how beloved he was by his own people. But before he could reply, Beowulf spoke again.

"Go quickly, Wiglaf, and find the treasures that lie inside of the barrow. There's no danger now, and you may enter safely. Examine the hoard and let me see the ancient heirlooms that the dragon has guarded for so many years. It would please me to see these great treasures that I will give to my people before I leave this life."

Although Wiglaf did not want to leave his king alone, he went at once to the entrance of the barrow. He made his way past the mighty arches and into the center of the mound. He stared in wonder at the piles of gold and other treasures filling the cavern. He'd never seen such riches gathered together in one place before. Heaps of necklaces and bracelets of

twisted gold, golden cups, and jewels lay there. Overhead, hung high above the piles of treasures, was a great banner spun from gold. It glittered and gleamed in the dim light so that Wiglaf could see into the far corners of the cavern. He gathered

together some of the finest pieces from the treasure hoard and turned to hurry back to his king, afraid that Beowulf might already be dead.

When he reached the bank where Beowulf was lying, Wiglaf saw that the frightened warriors who had fled from the battle had now left the shelter of the woods. With their shields and swords, they stood

close to Beowulf. They looked first at the old dying king and then at Wiglaf, with dishonor in their faces. They turned away their heads in shame.

Wiglaf spoke to them. "Those who know the truth will tell how this noble king had to defend himself when he was in great danger. I felt fear, but I did not flee. Although there was little I could do, I struck at the dragon with my sword and helped stop the power of its flames. But I alone couldn't save him. The story of your flight, your refusal to help your lord, will be told in countries far away. It will be many years before this is forgotten, and I wouldn't like the life of shame that you must now face."

Then Wiglaf ordered the men to stand aside so that he alone was with the king. He wiped the old warrior's face again, and Beowulf revived a little. Wiglaf raised him up in his arms.

"See the treasures that I've spread before you," he said. "This is just a small part of the hoard lying inside of the barrow."

Beowulf opened his eyes and looked at the pieces from the dragon's hoard that his thane had laid on the ground. "I'm glad I have won these treasures for my people," he said.

The old king looked at Wiglaf. "You are the last of my kinsmen, Wiglaf. I do not know who will guide our people when I'm gone, but if you are chosen, I ask that you rule wisely for as long as you are given life."

Beowulf paused and looked around him for the last time. "Wiglaf, see that great headland beyond the cliff's edge? Go to our people and command them to build a mighty barrow there—a mound that will be seen towering over the ocean. Seafarers will know it as a beacon when they sail over the great whale way toward our land, and it will be known as the Barrow of Beowulf."

Then Beowulf unclasped a golden collar from around his neck and presented it to the young thane.

"Take this, brave and dear kinsman, and may it bring you good fortune for the rest of your days." Beowulf had spoken his last words.

THE DRAGON'S END

iglaf saw that Beowulf was dead. Heavy with grief and exhaustion, he sat next to his dead king. All around him he could see the sea birds and hear their cries as they swooped and flew around the cliff's edge. They did not know that Beowulf, the greatest of men, was dead. Farther along the cliff lay the great dragon, no longer able to bring terror to the people from out of the night skies. The dragon, like Beowulf, had reached the end of its fleeting life.

After several minutes, Wiglaf slowly rose to his feet. The other warriors were gone, except for two or three men who had seen the glow of the dragon's flames and had gathered nearby. They stared uncertainly at Wiglaf and at where Beowulf lay. Wiglaf called to them and ordered that news of the battle should be carried to every corner of the nation. The men hurried to do as Wiglaf had commanded.

The story of Beowulf's slaying of the dragon, the bravery of Wiglaf, and Beowulf's death quickly spread throughout the land. A great crowd of people gathered on the cliff and quietly mourned for Beowulf. They stared in horror at the mighty dragon's body lying on ground scorched black by its fire. One bold man walked along the length of the dragon and declared that it was 50 paces long! The dragon had not been saved by the treasures that it guarded. Neither had the treasure brought it any good fortune.

Wiglaf turned to speak to the waiting people. "There are new riches lying inside this mound, but they've brought us nothing but sorrow. They have caused the death of our beloved king, Beowulf. Maybe in time they will bring us joy. Fate will decide. I have seen the dragon's hoard lying inside. Come, I'll show you the way through the passage so that we may collect the treasure. Then you, too, may see the wonder of it."

Carts were brought, and Wiglaf led some of the men to the hidden entrance of the ancient barrow. He carried a flaming torch in front, and the men followed him into the center of the mound. They searched through the cave until all of the treasures were gathered, and they carefully loaded them onto the carts. Then they pulled the laden carts back through the passage and out onto the cliff top.

Wiglaf called for the strongest men. "Now, you must push the body of the dragon over the cliff," he told them. "Thanks to our king, Beowulf, it will never again bring terror to our land. Let the ocean's currents take it and do with it what they will!"

The men fastened ropes around the dead creature's body. Watched by the crowd of people, they tugged at the ropes and slowly pulled the monster across the blackened grass toward the cliff's edge. The people saw its huge head and its great wings and claws. Some of them wept as they remembered the night of terror that it had brought them. When the dragon's body lay on the brink of the cliff, the men let go of the ropes and stood behind the body, ready to push it over the edge. Then with one heave, they sent it tumbling down into the waves. Some of the people peered at the surging

waves far below and saw the dragon's body as it was caught by the tides and slowly vanished from sight. A great sigh arose from the watching Geats, and a murmur of thankfulness ran through the crowd. They knew now that this terror could never return. They knew their noble king had saved them, and they gave thanks that Beowulf had killed the evil dragon.

BEOWULF'S BARROW

It was time to carry out Beowulf's last wishes and to arrange his funeral according to the customs of the country. Wiglaf ordered men to gather firewood and carry it to the headland that Beowulf had chosen. Willingly, the Geats scattered far and wide and gathered together a giant pile of wood. They built a magnificent funeral pyre, and around it they hung helmets, shields, and coats of armor. It was a funeral pyre worthy of their great king.

Gently, they laid the body of their dead king upon a bier, and four men carried it across the grassy slopes to the pyre. A procession of men and women formed behind Wiglaf. The voices of grieving women were heard raised in a song of sorrow, a dirge lamenting the loss of their leader.

This sound mixed with the sound of people's cries as the Geats mourned the death of their king. Everybody gathered around the pyre to watch. A flame was lit, and the wood began to crackle as the fire caught hold. Smoke billowed into the sky, black over the red of the roaring fire. It was carried by the winds up to the heavens.

When the flames had died down, the people started to build an earth mound around the ashes of the pyre. It rose high and broad on the headland, as Beowulf had asked. For ten days the people toiled at their work until this great monument was completed.

Then, for the last time, the people of the Geats gathered together to honor Beowulf. They watched as

Beowulf's thanes rode on their fine horses around and around the barrow. They joined in the singing as minstrels sang about the bravery of the old warrior and his great deeds. They honored him as one of the world's bravest and most courteous of men—one who was most kind to his people. They were glad that Beowulf's life had been a noble one and that his death had been honorable.

Finally, within Beowulf's barrow men placed some of the treasures from the dragon's hoard—golden rings and jewels—back under the ground. They let the earth have back some of the treasures that Beowulf had won for them at his death.

There it still lies to this day.

AFTERWORD

This story of Beowulf is a retelling of an ancient poem that was written in Old English. The poem survives in one manuscript that is believed to have been written around A.D. 1000, although the poem itself was certainly composed earlier.

Beowulf and his people, the Geats, lived in the part of Europe that is today in southern Sweden. The Spear-Danes, as their name suggests, lived in Denmark. It is not certain if Beowulf himself was a real person. He is probably intended to be an ideal hero of that time. Although many of Beowulf's adventures must be myths, there is enough information in the poem to make us wonder where myth and history meet. For example, some of the names that the poet mentions in Beowulf are known to have lived, including King Hygelac—Beowulf's uncle, who really was killed in a battle around A.D. 521.

The story of how this one manuscript survived is almost as exciting as the story of Beowulf itself. The one surviving manuscript is bound in a book that is kept in the British Library in London, England, and this book once belonged to a man named Sir Robert Cotton, who died in 1631. Before Sir Robert owned it, the manuscript probably belonged to a monastery, perhaps close to Lichfield, in Staffordshire, England. The signature of a dean of Lichfield, Laurence Nowell, is written on one of the pages of *Beowulf* and dated 1563. It was earlier than this in the 1500s that many monasteries and their libraries were destroyed by the order of Henry VIII, and yet somehow this manuscript survived. Perhaps it was hidden by its owner when the soldiers came to burn his library.

Then, having survived so many centuries, it was almost destroyed in a disastrous fire in 1731. At this time the book was stored in a house called Ashburnham House, close to Westminster Abbey, in London, England. The *Beowulf* manuscript was burned at the edges, and over the years these edges have crumbled in places. Fortunately, a scholar made a copy of the poem before too many of the words broke away, and it is this copy that today's readers must rely on for some of the missing words.

The story of *Beowulf* is an exciting one, with its tales of monsters and dragons and noble warriors. It also gives us a good idea of what was important to these early people. For example, men were expected to be completely loyal to their lord, and they would try to win honor for themselves and their lord through their behavior. In return, the lords would celebrate their victories with great feasts. There would be a lot of eating and drinking in great halls, and minstrels would sing about the glories of victory. It was also very important that the lord would give out gold and treasures to his loyal men, as well as ancient armor and swords, which were often given names.

And at this time there was a strong belief in fate that governed everything and everybody in this "fleeting" life.

Beowulf, the mighty warrior, deserves his place among the other ancient heroes whose adventures are enjoyed by both young and old.